For Michael, who knows the pleasures of a good nap

—R. M.

Rabbit Ears Books is an imprint of Rabbit Ears Productions, Inc.
Published by Simon & Schuster, Inc.
1230 Avenue of the Americas
New York, New York 10020

Manufactured in the United States of America.
2 4 6 8 10 9 7 5 3 1

Library of Congress Cataloging-in-Publication Data
Meyerowitz, Rick.
Rip Van Winkle / written by Washington Irving;
adapted and illustrated by Rick Meyerowitz.
p.   cm.
Summary: A man who sleeps for twenty years in the Catskill Mountains
awakes to a much-changed world.
ISBN: 0-689-80193-9
[1. Catskill Mountains Region (N.Y.)—Fiction.   2. New York (State)—Fiction.]
I. Irving, Washington, 1783-1859.   Rip Van Winkle.   II. Title.
PZ7.M5717554Ri 1995 [Fic]—dc20 94-48134

RIP VAN WINKLE

Written by **Washington Irving**

Adapted and Illustrated by **Rick Meyerowitz**

Rabbit Ears Books

It was the age of discovery and exploration. In the year 1609 Henry Hudson, commanding the Dutch ship *Half Moon,* sailed into what is now known as New York Harbor. There he discovered a great river. Determined to explore it, he sailed north until he came to the mysterious Catskill Mountains. He and his crew paused there to marvel at the landscape around them. They declared it to be the most beautiful on earth, and took an oath that wherever their travels would lead them, they would return to this fair place.

They journeyed on, sailing their little ship ever northward until they disappeared near the frozen top of the world. The way history books tell the story, Henry Hudson and his men were never seen again and never returned to those magical mountains or to the river that now bears his name.

But there is more than one way to tell a story.

Many years ago, when the country was still ruled by England, there lived a simple, good-natured though lazy fellow called Rip Van Winkle.

"Rip Van Winkle! Rip Van Winkle! Get out of bed! It's past noon! Your children are hungry! Your field needs plowing! And I need some help! Oh, why did I ever marry you?

I swear, you are the laziest man who ever walked in shoes! Rip Van Winkle, you are sleeping your life away!"

Dame Van Winkle was upset again. Years of not having food to put on the table, only rags in which to dress Rip, Jr., and little Sarah, and hard work day in and day out—while Rip was fishing, or napping, or off with his friends—had sharpened her anger.

Rip shrugged his shoulders and smiled sheepishly. Sarah, her golden curls bouncing like bedsprings, hid in the empty cupboard with their dog, Wolf. Rip, Jr., the spitting image of his father, napped contentedly, snoring away in the empty apple barrel. Rip's silence provoked his wife even further.

"You're not good for anything!" She unleashed a barrage of threats and complaints that drove Rip to the only side of the house where he was comfortable: the outside.

"Well, Wolf," said Rip, "now that we're out, why don't we walk down to the inn, and see what's new?"

Dusting himself off and whistling just a bit foolishly, he set off for the center of the village. Rip Van Winkle didn't like to work—everyone knew that—but he wasn't a bad man. He was well liked in the village, especially by the children. In part, this was because he was the best teller of tales in the neighborhood. He could make up a story that would frighten the fins off a fish, or tickle the berries off a fresh-baked pie. Children would surround him as he walked, tugging on his coat and clambering on his back. "Tell us a story, Rip," they would cry, and Rip usually would.

But today he walked unimpeded to the inn, and was greeted there by his friends: Nicholas Van Shicker, the innkeeper; Jacob Vinderbox, the schoolmaster; and old Peter Vonderlust. They gathered every day in front of the inn under the sign of King George III. They sat in the shade, drinking ale, chewing over old gossip, and telling endless sleepy stories they'd all heard before. Rip took his seat on the bench, and was just getting settled, when his wife burst in upon the tranquil group.

"I knew I'd find you here," she yelled, "wasting your afternoon away in the company of loafers. Our cupboard is bare, Husband. We've got nothing for dinner. The woods are filled with game. Here is your gun and pack. Don't come home again until you've got something to show for yourself."

With that, Dame Van Winkle spun on her heels, and, driving her anger before her like a flock of geese, stormed down the road.

There was no escaping this assignment. Rip sighed, bid farewell to his friends, and soon was trekking upward in the sunlit mountains.

Late in the afternoon, in a part of the country unfamiliar to him, he lay down to rest on a green knoll. From there Rip could see the silvery Hudson far, far below, moving on its silent and majestic course. In the other direction he looked into a deep shadowed mountain glen: wild, lonely, and rugged. Rip lay on his back lost in thought. The mountains began to throw their tall blue shadows over the valleys. It would be dark long before he could reach the village.

"Don't come home," she had said, "until you have something to show for yourself."

I have nothing, he thought. *Not even a squirrel for the table. How can I go home now?*

Suddenly, he heard a voice calling.

"Rip Van Winkle!"

He looked around, but saw no one.

"Rip Van Winkle! Rip Van Winkle!"

There it was again. With a low growl, Wolf jumped to his master's side. Rip looked down into the glen, and saw a strange figure slowly climbing toward him, carrying a heavy load.

The stranger was a grizzled fellow, dressed in the old Dutch style. He carried a stout wooden keg full of ale, and made signs for Rip to assist him with the load. Rip took the keg from him, and followed him up the narrow gully. He heard long rolling peals like distant thunder coming from a cleft in the lofty rocks toward which they climbed.

They passed through the opening and came to a hollow, like a small amphitheater, surrounded by tall cliffs. In the center was a company of most peculiar-looking men, with old-fashioned clothing and odd faces. They were playing at ninepins. With each roll of the ball, thunder echoed throughout the mountains.

One, taller than the rest, seemed to be the commander. Tucked into his belt were two pistols with carved handles, and from it dangled a long sword. He held up his hand, and the sound of mountain thunder fell silent. The men gathered around Rip, and stared at him with such stern gazes that his heart flip-flopped and his knees banged together like spoons on a clothesline. The commander beckoned him to pour from the keg. Rip obeyed, emptying the contents into heavy old flagons produced by the company. The men silently quaffed their ale, and went back to the game.

The commander pointed to a silver flagon, which had mysteriously appeared in Rip's hand, and ordered him to drink. Rip didn't think it was a good idea, but he didn't want to be impolite. So, with a nervous little laugh, he raised the flagon to his lips and drank.

It was rich and bubbly, thick with the scent of barley malts and sugars. A strong old drink. Too strong for him. He felt unsteady on his feet as if he were on a ship in a rough sea. The whole world was spinning around him. He heard the crash and roll of thunder. His eyes whirled in his head. The ground disappeared and he was falling through space. The commander was tumbling after him, faster and faster, almost upon him. He reached out to take the flagon from Rip's hand. Lightning flashed and thunder rolled. Rip shut his eyes tightly, and covered his ears with his hands.

I wish I weren't seeing this! he thought. *I wish I weren't hearing this! I wish I were asleep!* Blackness encircled him, and he got his wish, falling into the deepest sleep he, or anyone else, had ever had.

He slept all night, and all the next day, and each day after. Week followed week. Leaves fell from the trees, and the seasons changed. Snow blanketed him.

He slept on and on. Great events passed him by. The pages of history, turning slowly, began a new chapter without Rip Van Winkle.

Then one morning he awoke. Birds were hopping and twittering among the bushes, and an eagle was wheeling across the azure sky, soaring on the pure mountain breeze. He was on the green knoll where he had met the strange old man. *Surely, I haven't slept here all night,* thought Rip.

He looked around for his flintlock, but in its place found a rusty old gun. Wolf, too, was gone. He whistled after him, and shouted his name, but no dog appeared. Rip felt quite stiff. Something was digging into his back . . . the flagon! It was tarnished and dented, but it was very definitely the same one from last night.

"Oh, you wicked, wicked flagon," said Rip.

He decided to return to the clearing to ask for his gun and dog. But on retracing his path of the night before, he was surprised to find a mountain stream foaming down the gully. With some difficulty he reached the place where the opening in the cliffs had been.

Imagine his astonishment when he discovered no trace of the clearing or of the strange men. Only a high, impenetrable wall of rock over which the stream came tumbling in a sheet of feathery foam.

What was to be done? He couldn't stay here, but he dreaded meeting his wife. He shook his head, shouldered the rusty old flintlock, and with a heart full of trouble and strife, turned toward home.

As he approached the village, he met a number of people he didn't recognize. This surprised him, for he thought he knew everyone. They, in turn, all stared at him, and stroked their chins so thoughtfully and often that Rip found himself doing the same.

To his amazement he discovered he had grown a beard ten feet long! *How could this be?* he thought. *It's as if I haven't shaved for twenty years.*

He entered the outskirts of the village. A troop of unfamiliar children ran at his heels, pointing rude little fingers, hooting and laughing at him. The very village had changed. There were rows of houses he had never seen before, and other houses had disappeared. Was he losing his mind? Surely this was his own village, which he had left only the day before. *Those wicked men have played a trick on me,* he thought, *and their ale has boggled my brain.*

He found the way to his own house, and approached it with dread. He expected at any moment to hear the angry, accusing voice of Dame Van Winkle. "Don't come home until you've got something to show for yourself," she had said.

"I've lost everything, and all I've got to show for it is this beat-up old flagon. I'm no good to anyone," wailed Rip. "No good at all. I'll change, Wife. I promise. From now on I'll work harder than any man."

Rip tried to open the door, but it came off its hinges. His house was falling apart! The roof had caved in, and the windows were shattered. He called loudly for his wife and children. The lonely rooms echoed his call, then were silent.

He hurried to the village inn. A large, new building, the Union Hotel, stood in its place. From the top of a white flagpole fluttered an unfamiliar banner of stars and stripes. Even the portrait of King George was different. There was a bustling, busy crowd about the place, and the appearance of Rip with his rusty gun, and ancient, torn clothes, attracted immediate attention.

One man asked on which side he would vote. Another fellow inquired whether he was a Federal or Democrat. Rip was at a loss to answer. He didn't even understand the questions.

"Alas! Gentlemen," said Rip, "I am a poor, quiet man, a native of this village, and a loyal subject of King George, bless him!"

A great shout burst from the bystanders. "Spy! A spy! Arrest him!"

Rip was alarmed. "I mean no harm," he cried. "I came in search of my friends and neighbors. Where's Nicholas Van Shicker?"

A man replied, "The old innkeeper? Why he's dead and gone eighteen years now."

"Where's Jacob Vinderbox, the schoolmaster?"

"He became a great general in the war, and is now in Congress," answered another.

Every answer puzzled Rip. Such enormous lapses of time! And things he could not understand. War? Congress? He cried out in despair, "Does nobody here know Rip Van Winkle?"

"Oh, Rip Van Winkle!" they all exclaimed. "Sure. There's Rip Van Winkle, leaning against the tree." Rip looked, and beheld a perfect copy of himself as he was when he went up the mountain.

"If that's Rip Van Winkle over there, then who am I? Not myself. Somebody else, for sure. I was myself when I fell asleep on the mountain. Now everything is changed and I'm not me. I don't know who I am!"

At that moment Rip spotted a lively young woman with a head full of golden curls. She held a chubby child in her arms, who, frightened by Rip's long white beard, began to cry.

"Hush, Little Rip. Hush, little boy. The old man won't hurt you," she said.

The name of the child, the way the mother looked and spoke, pierced poor Rip's heart.

"Tell me . . . what is your name, young woman?" he asked.

"My name is Sarah Gardener."

"And your father's name?"

"Ah, my father. Rip Van Winkle was his name. It's been twenty years since he went away from home. His dog came home without him, and we searched the country all around. Nobody knows what happened to him. I was but a little girl then." Here she faltered, and brushed a tear from her cheek. "I am sad to say my brother and I grew up without him, and he was sorely missed."

Rip had one more question. With a shaking voice he asked, "And your mother? Where's your mother?"

"My mother," replied Sarah, "raised us herself, and seeing us full grown, decided on a change of life. It has been two years since she married a traveling peddler, and traveled with him to South America."

Rip could contain himself no longer. He caught Sarah and her child in his arms.

"I am your father!" he cried. "Young Rip Van Winkle once. Wrinkled Rip Van Winkle now! Does no one know me?"

A voice called out, "I do." It was old Peter Vonderlust. He remembered Rip at once.

"Rip Van Winkle, old friend, where have you been all this time?" Rip told his story and all were amazed. None more so than Rip himself, to whom twenty years had seemed to be one night.

There were some doubters, but they were quieted by Peter Vonderlust. "It's a fact," he said. "The Catskills are haunted. The spirits of Henry Hudson and his crew keep watch over the river and mountains every twenty years. My father once saw them in their old Dutch costume, playing at ninepins in a mountain hollow."

To make a long story short, the crowd broke up and returned to its business. Sarah took Rip home to live with her.

She had a snug, well-furnished house, and a stout, cheery farmer for a husband, whom Rip remembered as one of the boys who used to climb upon his back. As to Rip, Jr., he was the very image of his father. He could never be found when there was work to be done. And now that Rip wanted to work, he discovered that no one expected him to. Having nothing to do at home, he took his place on the bench by the oak tree in front of the hotel.

Catching up on events, he learned there had been a revolutionary war, that the country had overthrown the rule of old England, and that he was now a free citizen of the United States of America. Bless them one and all!

He became quite a celebrity. People came from far and wide to hear him tell his story. And tell it he did. Over and over. At first it varied a bit. Doubtless this was because he had only recently awakened. At last, it settled down precisely to the tale I have just related, and every man, woman, and child in the village knew it by heart. There were some who still doubted the truth of it. The old Dutch inhabitants, however, gave it full credit. Even to this day they never hear a thunderstorm in the Catskills without saying that Henry Hudson and his crew are playing at ninepins.